I'M NOT A GIRL

Written by
Maddox Lyons & Jessica Verdi

Illustrated by
Dana Simpson

ROARING BROOK PRESS
NEW YORK

Today is picture day.
I hate picture day.

But nobody understands.
"You look so pretty in this,"
Mom tells me.

I don't want to be pretty.
Not on picture day.
And not on Halloween either.
"How about a princess gown?"
the salesperson asks. "Or fairy wings?"

Finally, I find the perfect costume.

"A pirate it is, matey!" But Mom takes
a different costume off the rack.

Beth comes over to trick or treat.

"How come *you* get to dress like a boy?" I grumble.

She shrugs. "My mom says she used to be a tomboy too."

"What's a tomboy?"

"A girl who likes boyish stuff."

Oh. That's not me then.
"I'm not a girl," I tell her.
Beth looks confused.
"I'm not a girl," I say again,
taking out my sword.
Beth draws her sword too.

Nobody seems to hear me,
so I try to show them
what I mean.

But that doesn't work either.

When it snows, Dad and I go outside to play.
"Honey, put on your jacket," he tells me.

I flop down into the snow and make another angel.
I'd rather be cold and wet than not be me.

There are so many amazing
women who have accomplished
so many important things.

I *know* girls are really cool.

RENÉE RICHARDS

I'm just not one.

I've spent all year wishing, but birthday wishes are the most powerful. I close my eyes and feel the warmth from the candles on my face.

I wish...everyone saw the real me.

I keep the wish in my mind, even after my birthday is over. Summer comes, and I have to go shopping again. But I can't stay quiet this time.

I say "No, no, no, **NO**!" to every swimsuit Mom picks.

"We're not leaving until you pick something," she says.

"Anything."

I can tell she's frustrated.

But all year, I've felt frustrated too.

"Anything?" I ask. "You mean it?"
Mom nods.

"Well, it will protect you from the sun..."

I meet two new friends at the pool.

We spend the day playing games, having races,

and timing how long we can hold our breath underwater.

"Time to reapply your sunscreen, Hannah," Dad calls.
"Hannah?" Grace says, confused.

"We thought you were a boy," Jake says.
"I *am* a boy," I insist. "No one believes me though."

"We believe you," Grace says, nodding.

"You're like our cousin. Our family thought she was a boy, but she's actually a girl," Jake says. "She's transgender."

I think about what Grace
and Jake said.

Over the next few days,
I gather up my courage.

And when Mom and Dad and I are having breakfast together, I start to talk.

I talk and talk and talk.

I say all the things I didn't know how to say before.

I tell them I'm a boy.

Mom and Dad both listen.

Finally, there's only one thing left to say.
"Can I get a haircut?"

This year, I'm excited for picture day.

A Mother's Note Twelve years ago, I gave birth to a baby I thought was a girl. Starting when our child was seven, he tried to show us, just like Hannah in the book, that in his heart and in his brain, he was a boy. When he was nine, he learned the word for this: *transgender*.

In childhood, girls may play with cars, or boys may play with dolls. Girls may not like wearing dresses, and boys may want their nails painted. Some degree of gender-nonconforming behavior is common and does not indicate that a child is transgender. What makes transgender children different from their peers is their insistence on a gender identity they were not assigned at birth.

Once we understood what our child had been trying to tell us, his dad and I helped him socially transition. He picked a new name, got "boys" clothing, changed his pronouns to he/him/his, and finally (finally!), he got a short haircut.

After my son came out to us, we went in search of children's books for and about kids like him. There were very few, so my son set out to write one. *I'm Not a Girl* is his story.

—Rachel Q. Lyons

Author's Note Seeing oneself reflected in the pages of a book is essential—for all of us, but especially for children who may not yet have the words or courage to explain what they're going through. This is why I strive to write about identity and acceptance in books for kids of all ages, and why I'm honored to have collaborated on this wonderful, necessary project with Maddox Lyons and his family.

—Jessica Verdi

Illustrator's Note It was an honor and a privilege, being asked to work on this book.

I'm a transgender woman myself. I was assigned "boy" as a birth gender. That was wrong. So, eventually, I had to work up the courage to tell my parents I was a girl. And while I was a bit older than the main character in this book, I know how it feels to do that.

I was nervous. Nervous to be honest about who I was inside and ask the people who loved me most in the world to see me as my real self and accept me for it. And I was terrified that they wouldn't.

My parents were great about it, a lot like Hannah's parents. And that means so much, for a kid of any age. I've been closer to my parents since that day. Unconditional love and acceptance are powerful things. And being accepted for who I was helped me to go on and do all the other things I wanted to do in life.

I hope this book helps other transgender kids and their families understand each other. Everybody should get to be who they are.

—Dana Simpson

A Note from the Creators

While reading *I'm Not a Girl*, you may have noticed the illustration of athlete and transgender activist Renée Richards on Hannah's classroom wall. Though a majority of school curriculums still focus on cisgender (non-trans) figures from history, we felt it was important to feature a transgender woman in the Women's History Month scene, as a call to educators and publishers to include the transgender community in course materials and lesson plans. Representation matters!

There are many transgender individuals (women and men, as well as nonbinary people) whom we recommend looking up for further learning. Here are just a few:

Charley Parkhurst (1812–1879) was a nineteenth-century farmer, rancher, and stagecoach driver.

Alan L. Hart (1890–1962) was a physician and medical researcher.

Billy Tipton (1914–1989) was an accomplished jazz musician.

Renée Richards (1934–) is an eye surgeon, veteran, athlete, and tennis coach who won a landmark case for transgender rights.

Lou Sullivan (1951–1991) was an author and activist.

Sylvia Rivera (1951–2002) was the cofounder of Street Transvestite Action Revolutionaries (STAR), an organization dedicated to helping homeless LGBTQIA+ youth and transgender women.

Kylar Broadus (1963–) is an attorney, activist, public speaker, author, and professor.

Jill Soloway (1965–) is a nonbinary award-winning writer, director, and producer.

Chaz Bono (1969–) is a writer, musician, and actor.

Laverne Cox (1972–) is an actress and the first openly transgender person to be nominated for a Primetime Emmy Award for acting.

Janet Mock (1983–) is an author, television and podcast host, director, producer, and transgender rights activist.

Danica Roem (1984–) is a journalist and politician and the first openly transgender person to serve in a U.S. state legislature.

Jonathan Van Ness (1987–) is a nonbinary hair stylist, podcaster, and television personality.

Jaiyah Saelua (1988–) is the first transgender woman to play in the soccer World Cup.

Sarah McBride (1990–) is an activist and the first openly transgender person to speak at a major American political party convention.

Jazz Jennings (2000–) is a YouTube and television personality, college student, and LGBTQIA+ rights activist.

Resources We Recommend

Books for children
Red: A Crayon's Story by Michael Hall
It Feels Good to Be Yourself: A Book About Gender Identity by Theresa Thorn; illustrations by Noah Grigni
I Am Jazz by Jessica Herthel and Jazz Jennings; illustrations by Shelagh McNicholas

Books for adults
Raising the Transgender Child: A Complete Guide for Parents, Families, and Caregivers
      by Michele Angello and Ali Bowman
The Transgender Child: A Handbook for Families and Professionals by Stephanie Brill and Rachel Pepper
Parenting Beyond Pink & Blue: How to Raise Your Kids Free of Gender Stereotypes
      by Christia Spears Brown

Media for the family
Gender Revolution: A Journey with Katie Couric (2017; National Geographic)
The Most Dangerous Year (2018; Dangerous Year Productions)
Raising Ryland (2015; CNN Films)
The Real Thing (2017; bRandom Media)
How to Be a Girl (podcast; Marlo Mack)

Organizations
Human Rights Campaign (hrc.org)
GLAAD (glaad.org)
PFLAG (pflag.org)
GLSEN (glsen.org)
Gender Spectrum (genderspectrum.org)
The Trevor Project (thetrevorproject.org)
Trans Youth Equality Foundation
      (transyouthequality.org)
TransFamily Support Services
      (transfamilysos.org)